Where You Came From

SARA O'LEARY

with illustrations by

JULIE MORSTAD

First paperback edition published in 2020. First published in 2008.
www.simplyreadbooks.com

Text © 2008 Sara O'Leary
Illustrations © 2008 Julie Morstad

Library and Archives Canada Cataloguing in Publication
O'Leary, Sara
        Where you came from / Sara O'Leary ; pictures by Julie Morstad.
ISBN 978-1-77229-016-5 (paperback)
ISBN 978-1-894965-46-0 (hard cover)
        I. Morstad, Julie II. Title.
PS8579.L293W48 2007   jC813'.54   C2007-905128-6

We gratefully acknowledge the suppport of the Canada Council of the Arts, the
Government of Canada through the Book Publishing Industry Development Program
and the BC Arts Council for our publishing program.

Book design by Robin Mitchell Cranfield for hundreds & thousands

Printed in Korea

10 9 8 7 6 5 4 3 2 1

Where You Came From

SARA O'LEARY

with illreflightprefions by

JULIE MORSTAD

Simply Read Books

Henry is a boy who likes to ask questions.
Every day it's something new.

Do one and one always make two? he asks.
And never something more?

But there is one particular question
he asks again and again.

Where did I come from? asks Henry.

Well, says his father.

It was so long ago now
that it is difficult to remember.

I think that was the day
that the stork called in sick,
and a flock of crows
took over his deliveries.

No, says his mother.
Don't you remember?

The fairies brought you.

It must have taken dozens
of them to lift you,
because they were so small
and you were so big.

No, says his father.
Don't you remember?

We found you in a basket,
floating down the river.

We'd been out for a picnic
and it was the perfect end
to a perfect blue-sky day.

No, says his mother.
Don't you remember?

One night we looked up in the sky
and saw a falling star.

We wished on it,
and when it got close to earth,
we saw you riding on its tail.

No, says his father.
Don't you remember?

It was a spaceship, not a star.
It was round and silver
and we'd never seen anything like it.

Then the door opened
and you fell to earth.

No, says his mother.
Don't you remember?

Your father got you in the mail.
Special delivery.

And since there was no return address,
we decided to keep you.

No, says his father.
Don't you remember?

Your mother found you
at the supermarket.

She says she has no idea
why you were in the sale bin.
There was absolutely nothing wrong with you.

No, says his mother.
Don't you remember?

Your father spotted you in an eagle's nest
when we were out walking in the forest.

He saw you there, way up high.
We couldn't leave you there all alone,
so your father climbed up and got you.

no, says his father.
Don't you remember?

Passing a pet store, one day,
your mother saw you in the window.

You were the friskiest of all the puppies,
and she knew she had to have you.

No, says his mother.
Don't you remember?

Your father saw a red balloon appear,
far off in the sky.

And at the end of the string,
there you were,
holding on for dear life.

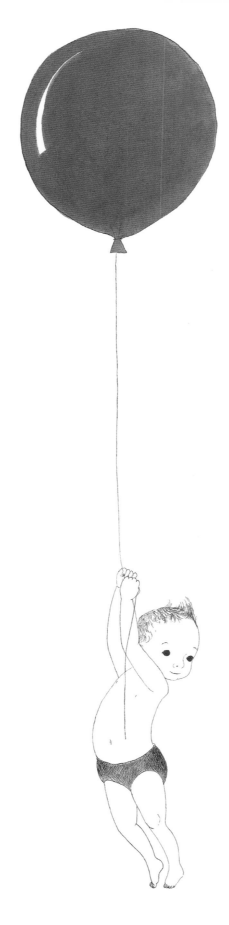

No, says his father.
Don't you remember?

Your mother grew you in her garden.

She said the hardest part was waiting,
being patient, stopping herself
from picking you too soon.

No, says his mother.
Don't you remember?

Your father made you in his workshop.
He carved you out of wood.
It took weeks.

And we loved you
just like you were a real little boy.

Oh, says his father, I remember.
It wasn't like that at all.

It was quite simple.

Your mother and I both dreamt you.
And then you came true.

That's where I came from? asks Henry.

You dreamt of a baby
and the baby you dreamed became me?

Oh yes, says his mother.
I remember perfectly now.

First there were two of us and then we were three.

 THE END

THE HENRY BOOKS

When You Were Small

Where You Came From

When I Was Small